This Little Tiger book belongs to:

_____

_____

_____

For Jack and Joe Mongredien,
and their very special Grandpa – S M

For Anne and Paul, with love – C B

LITTLE TIGER PRESS

1 The Coda Centre, 189 Munster Road, London SW6 6AW
www.littletiger.co.uk

First published in Great Britain 2011
This edition published 2016

Text copyright © Sue Mongredien 2011
Illustrations copyright © Cee Biscoe 2011

Sue Mongredien and Cee Biscoe have asserted their rights
to be identified as the author and illustrator of this work under
the Copyright, Designs and Patents Act, 1988

Printed in China

2 4 6 8 10 9 7 5 3 1

Before We Go To Bed

Sue
Mongredien

Cee
Biscoe

LITTLE TIGER PRESS
London

Barney and Grandpa Bear were tramping
home together after a busy day.
"What are we going to do next?"
Barney asked.
"Next?" chuckled Grandpa in surprise.
"Next, I think it's bedtime, Barney!"

Grandpa pulled off Barney's boots
with a heave-squelch-plop!
    "Now, let's get you ready for
bed," he said.

"Not yet, Grandpa!" Barney cried. "I ALWAYS have a GIANT bowl of oatmeal before I go to bed. Yummy, yummy oatmeal, with sticky, licky honey!"

"Are you sure?" asked Grandpa.

"Oh, yes," said Barney. "Come on!"

Barney showed Grandpa what a wonderful oatmeal-maker he was.

"And now for the honey!" he cheered. But the honey was runny . . . and it went EVERYWHERE.

"Whoops-a-daisy!" giggled Barney.

"Time for bed now," said Grandpa,
when Barney's tummy was full.

"But I ALWAYS have a big bubble bath before
I go to bed!" said Barney. "A splishy-sploshy
bath with my squeezy-squirty toys."

"I suppose you are a very sticky bear," Grandpa said, as Barney tipped in ALL the bubble bath with a glug-glug-gloop.

Barney splished and sploshed around
in his bubble bath. The water went
EVERYWHERE.

"Whoops-a-daisy!" giggled Barney.

"All clean!" Grandpa said. "It MUST be bedtime now."

"But I'll NEVER get to sleep without a story," Barney said. "A spooky, scare-a-bear story with horrible, hairy monsters."

"Is a spooky, scare-a-bear story a good idea before bed?" Grandpa wondered. "Don't worry, Grandpa," said Barney. "It's only a story. It's not real."

So Grandpa read the story.

Afterward, Grandpa put the light
on again to make them both feel better.

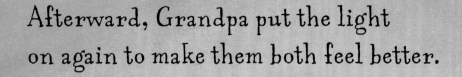

"Maybe we shouldn't go
to sleep just yet," he said.

"I've got an amazing idea," said Barney.
"We could bounce on the bed! Shall we, Grandpa?"

Grandpa smiled.
"All right then," he said.
First they did little bear bounces.

Next they did bigger
bear bounces.

And then they did
**great big,
springy-zingy,
boingy-bear
bounces!**

Until ...

Crash! went the bed.

"Whoops-a-daisy!"
said Barney and Grandpa.

Barney watched as Grandpa
mended the bed. Then he gave a
hu-u-uge stretchy yawn.

"Sounds to me like it's definitely bedtime,"
said Grandpa, tucking Barney under
the covers.

"There's just one more thing I need,"
said Barney sleepily. "A super-squeezy,
squishy-squashy . . ."

"...BEAR HUG!"

Then both bears fell fast asleep
until the morning.